Map of Norway provided by:
*www.worldatlas.com*

# Norse Mythology Who's Who

**Odin-** *In Norse Mythology, Odin was the god of wisdom, poetry, war and death. He carried a spear called "Grungir," that never missed its target. He gathered warriors who had died in battle to Valhalla, a great palace-like place where there was feasting and celebration. Odin was the head god in Aesir where the gods lived.*

**Freya-** *In Norse Mythology, Freya is the most beautiful and kindest of the Norse goddesses. She loves music, flowers, elves, and fairies. She lives in a beautiful palace called Flokvang. Freya married the god Od, who disappeared one day. She missed him so much that when she cried, her tears turned to gold.*

**Loki-** *In Norse Mythology, Loki was a trickster. He was always causing mischief and getting into trouble. Loki could change his shape. He was known to have become a horse or a wolf.*

**Asgard-** *One of the nine Mythological Norse worlds. It is where all the Aesir gods named above live.*

# The Tale
## · of the ·
# Troll's Horse

By Annie Jacobsen
Illustrated By Susan Jo Hanson

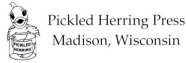

Pickled Herring Press
Madison, Wisconsin

# "THE TALE OF THE TROLL'S HORSE"

Written by Annie Jacobsen
Illustrated by Susan Jo Hanson

*The Author and Publisher wishes to thank her dear friend Susan for the many hours she spent on her beautiful illustrations, Cate Cody and Tommy for being her models, and Ruth Ann Lobacz and Jon Knutson for their editing and proof-reading support.*

*We would also like to thank Karen and Stuart Hanson of Yahara River Fjords, and Martha and Guy Martin for their wonderful pictures and help on this project.*

*A special thanks to Mike May and the Norwegian Fjord Horse Registry Board members for letting us use the information about the breed in our book.*

*The Pickled Herring Press Logo and name are trademarks of Annie Jacobsen and Susan Jo Hanson.*
*All rights reserved.*

No part of this book may be copied or reproduced in any way without the author's written consent.

® Copyright 2009  Contact: Ann Rouse  ~  *annies49@yahoo.com*
*www.pickledherringpress.com*  ~  Madison, Wisconsin

Library of Congress Control Number: 2008943437

Publisher's Cataloging-In-Publication Data
(Prepared by The Donohue Group, Inc.)
Jacobsen, Annie.
 The tale of the troll's horse / by Annie Jacobsen ; illustrated by Susan Jo Hanson.

 p. : ill. ; cm.

 Includes bibliographical references.
 Summary: The brave little mare Freya dreams of a beautiful black stallion named Odin, who has been carried off and placed under a spell by a twelve-headed troll. When Odin suddenly appears in the King's stable, Freya knows she must free the stallion from the evil spell, for Odin is her own true love.
 ISBN: 978-0-9778276-3-3

1. Horses--Juvenile fiction. 2. Trolls--Juvenile fiction. 3. Magic--Juvenile fiction. 4. Fairy tales. 5. Horses--Fiction. 6. Trolls--Fiction. 7. Magic--Fiction. 8. Fairy tales. I. Hanson, Susan Jo. II. Title.

PZ7.J33 Ta 2009
PS3610.A26 T35 2009
[E]                                                                                                                            2008943437

Printed and Bound in Hong Kong
*The ink used in this book was tested and found to be lead free.*

# Dedication

*This book is dedicated to all those patient horses and ponies everywhere who allow us to ride upon their strong backs and teach us many of life's most valuable lessons.*

*Most especially, we dedicate this book to the dear horses that we have loved and lost as well as those who currently enrich our lives and calm our souls.*

***Tracer***

***Buddy***

***Willie***

***Queenie***

***Cocoa***

***Mitzy***

***Tennessee***

***Tiny Puff***

***Mr. Sandman "Rusty"***

***Let's Burn a Debt "Bernie"***

***Desirable Beauty "Phyllis"***

***Idol of Greystone "Idol"***

***Ridgefield's Noble Lady "Lady"***

***Dreams Denied "D.D."***

***CH Molotov Foxtail "Molly"***

*God bless them all!*

One fine morning in the Voss Valley
As Siri the mare and her young foal Loki
Were led out through the pasture gate,
Loki asked a question that just wouldn't wait.

"Why do we have this black streak in our manes?"
"It is all of Odin, the Troll's horse, that remains."
Loki asked, "Who was Odin, and what did he do?"
"I know the story well," nickered Siri." I'll tell it to you."

Odin, the troll's steed, was fierce and brave.
He lived with a troll inside of a cave.
The troll held captive, princesses twelve
Until Ashlad saved them and himself as well.

When the troll was vanquished and the princesses freed,
They all rode home on the Terrible Troll's Steed.
Smoke and fire blew from his nostrils wide,
His hooves struck sparks on the mountain side.

There was a joyous celebration upon their safe return
And Ashlad wed the youngest princess 'mid flower and fern.
"What happened to Odin?" Loki cried.
"Just listen! I'll tell you," his mother replied.

"He was placed in the King's stable that very first night.
Odin's stomping and snorting gave the horses a fright.
His stall was next to a spunky, sturdy, little mare
With a neatly trimmed mane and honey gold hair.

Her name was Freya, after the Norse goddess of love
Who was married and widowed in Asgard above.
Freya belonged to the princess whom Ashlad had wed.
The mare was wise, courageous, and not easily misled.

Long before Odin had arrived on the scene,
Freya had begun to have a strange dream.
Three nights in a row her dream was the same,
Of a handsome black stallion, gentle and tame.

The stud had been taken by a huge Mountain Troll
Up to his cave in a high mountain knoll.
The troll had used a powerful spell
That made Odin huge and fire-breathing as well.

Freya recognized Odin as the horse in her dream.
He was the handsomest steed that she'd ever seen.
Though his fierce looks were not very inviting,
Freya knew in her heart he was much less frightening.

The others didn't understand and kept their distance,
Only Freya stayed near; she was fire resistant.
She must break the troll's spell to make Odin her own,
But who would help? She couldn't do it alone.

Freya thought of Thorvald the Nisse who guarded the farm.
He kept the crops growing and the animals from harm.
Only he knew how to break the troll's spell.
If she brought him an apple, perhaps he would tell.

She found Thorvald snoozing in a small manger.
He quickly awoke, sensing he was in danger.
When he recognized Freya, he said, "You gave me a start!
I thought you were that pesky cat that sleeps under the cart."

"What have you brought, little Freya, for my lunch?"
"I have brought a juicy red apple for you to munch.
Please help me break Odin's troll spell.
I know if you will, then all will be well."

The Nisse thanked Freya and then softly said,
"You must fetch apples: two green, two yellow, two red.
At the next full moon, over the King's orchard wall you must go.
Carefully pick two of the green apples Granny Smith loved so.

Quickly back over the wall to the stable you must flee.
Give one green apple to your true love, and bring the other to me."
Freya trotted quietly back to her stall to think and to plan.
Whispering, "I can do this, I can do this, I can do this, I can!"

On the very next evening when the moon was full and bright,
Freya leapt over the wall and saw a softly glowing light.
It appeared to be coming from a short, leafy, green tree,
Which whispered to Freya, "What need you from me?"

"Oh kind tree, to save my true love, I must break a troll's awful spell.
Please give me two of your green apples, and all will be well."
"Dear Freya," the green branches whispered above,
"I will give you the apples that Granny Smith loved."

"Thank you, dear tree, for your generous gift.
You surely have given my spirits a lift!
Now I must hurry for the day begins anew,"
So back over the wall with her apples she flew.

The Nisse was waiting for his green apple treat.
Freya laid the prized apple right at his feet.
"Well done little Freya; only two tasks to go;
Then Odin will be the kind horse you love so."

Tired and frightened, Freya arrived at Odin's door.
She gently laid the green apple on his stall floor.
Odin spied the apple and quickly gobbled it up.
Then to Freya's surprise, he let out a loud burp.

As she watched wide-eyed, the troll's spell faded.
He had shrunk five hands, and his temper abated.
Though smoke still blew out of his nose and ears,
Odin was calmer, and his eyes glistened with tears.

Freya noticed small changes as the days slowly passed.
Odin's snorting was softer, and his tantrums didn't last.
As the night of the next full moon drew ever nearer,
Freya's second task became increasingly clearer.

The Nisse had said to find two, delicious, golden apples.
She should look where the ground was moonlit and dappled.
As she flew at the orchard wall, it seemed to grow higher,
Still, she must not fail, or the results would be dire.

Freya's courage never faltered as up and over she went,
Straight toward a golden glow under branches old and bent.
"Oh please, kind tree, to save my true love and break the troll's spell,
I need two of your Golden Delicious apples, and all will be well."

"Dear Freya," the green branches whispered above,
"I will give you the apples for your own true love."
"Thank you, dear tree, for your generous gift.
You really have given my spirits a lift!"

Back over the wall with her apples Freya did fly,
One for the Nisse and one for Odin to try.
Again with head lowered, she approached the steed.
She laid down the apple which he gobbled with greed.

Odin gave a great burp just as he had before,
Then proceeded to shrink five hands or more.
He peered down at the mare with a thoughtful look,
But he didn't notice that her knees really shook.

When Freya returned to her stall, the Nisse was waiting.
"Well done, little mare; the troll's spell is disintegrating.
The final task will be dangerous and the most difficult.
You will have to have great courage to bring it about.

Two Ruby Red apples grow in the heart of the orchard.
They are guarded by the King's fierce hound, old Borchard.
He will give you the apples when the moon is new
If you can convince him that your love is true.

Just follow your instincts and your heart.
Borchard will see just how faithful you are.
Return with two Ruby Reds, one for my token,
The other for your love, and the spell will be broken."

The very next night as the moon turned new,
Freya knew exactly what she had to do.
She approached the wall surrounding her prize,
Which seemed to grow higher right in front of her eyes.

Without thought for her safety, she began to run.
Her sturdy legs carried her up and over in one.
She raced through the orchard to its very heart,
And what she found there really gave her a start.

There just in front of the ruby red tree,
Sat old Borchard as big as could be.
With fangs to his knees and bleary old eyes,
He looked to be twice little Freya's size.

"What is it you want, little Freya so yummy?
Tell me at once or you'll be filling my tummy."
"I've come for two apples, your Ruby Red kind,
To break the troll's spell on a true love of mine."

"What price would you pay to prove your love true?"
Freya said, "I'd lay down my life and give it to you!"
Borchard growled, "Your answer's the one that I needed to hear;
Here are your apples; you have nothing to fear."

Freya raced back to the high wall once more.
She flew over it easily and arrived at the door.
Old Thorvald was waiting, smiling and wise.
He gave Freya a pat as he claimed his Ruby Red prize.

Just as dawn was quietly breaking,
Freya approached Odin's stall on legs that were shaking.
Her head was held high; there was love in her eyes
As she laid at his feet the Ruby Red prize.

Odin gobbled up the apple, and to his surprise,
He'd become his old self and regained normal size.
"Dear Freya," he said, "I owe you my life!
You've broken the spell! Please be my wife!"

"Is that the end?" little Loki cried.
"Not quite, just listen," Siri sighed.
"I will tell you the rest, and then you will see
How the Fjord horse's black stripe came to be.

From Odin and Freya we have all come.
Some red, some grey, but mostly brown dun.
Our brave hearts come from Freya, the fearless gold mare,
Who saved her love Odin from the troll's evil snare.

The black stripe in our mane is Odin's legacy.
We wear it proudly now for everyone to see.
It is all that is left of the Terrible Troll's horse,
Who loved the mare Freya, for better or worse."

"So that's why we have the black stripe in our mane!
Now will you tell me how I got my name?"
"Oh Loki, you curious young colt," Siri replied,
"That's enough for today; come close to my side.

Here comes Johannah to bring us back home.
She's a kind, sweet, delightful little gnome.
Its time to go, there's no more to say."
I'll tell you that tale some other day.

# The Norwegian Fjord Horse

"The Norwegian Fjord Horse is one of the world's oldest and purest breeds. It is believed that the original Fjord Horse migrated to Norway and was domesticated over 4.000 years ago. Herds of wild Fjord Horses existed in Norway after the last ice age. Archaeological excavations at Viking burial sites indicate that the Fjord Horse has been selectively bred for at least 2,000 years."*

One of the most unique characteristics of the Fjord Horse is its mane. The center hair of the mane is usually black while the outer hair is white. The mane is trimmed short so the hair stands up and the black stripe can be easily seen.

Fjord Horses are quick learners and remember what they are taught. They have smooth balanced gaits that make them a pleasure to ride or drive. They are strong, sure-footed mounts for children and adults alike. The Fjord Horse's gentle disposition, obedient nature, and willing attitude make it an ideal family horse.

Most of the Fjord Horses are a brown dun color, like Freya in our story, but they can also be red dun, gray dun, yellow dun, or white dun. If you would like additional information about the breed or would like to see pictures of these types of Fjord Horses, you can visit the Norwegian Fjord Horse website at www.nfhr.com.

*Information taken from the Norwegian Fjord Horse Registry website. A special thank you to Mike May, Executive Director of the Norwegian Fjord Horse Registry and the Board of Directors for their permission to use this information for our book.*

*Photo courtesy of Yahara River Fjords*
*Karen and Stuart Hanson*

# More Scandinavian Horse Stories

"Fritz and the Beautiful Horses," Jan Brett, Houghton Mifflin Co., 1981. ISBN# 0-395-30850-X, Hardcover $16.95. ISBN# 0-395-45356-9, Paperback $5.95

"The Hat," Jan Brett, G.P. Putnam's Sons, 1997. ISBN# 0-399-23101-3, Hardcover $16.95

"A Ride on the Red Mare's Back," Ursula LeGuin, Orchard Paperbacks, 1996. ISBN# 0-531-07079-4, Paperback $6.95

"The Ice Ponies," Renne, Floris Books, 2002. ISBN# 0-86315-384-4, Hardcover $15.95

"Peter and the Troll Baby," Jan Wahl, Golden Books, 1994. ISBN# 978-30716525-6 *Price unknown*

"Per and the Dala Horse," Rebecca Hickox, Double Day, 1995. ISBN# 978-395-32075-2, Hardcover $15.95

"Old Lars," Erica Magnum, Erica Magnum, 1984. ISBN# 978-87614-253-6, *Price unknown*

"Magic Hoofbeats, Horse Tales From Many Lands," Josepha Sherman, Barefoot Books, 2004. ISBN# 1-84148-091-6, Price $19.99

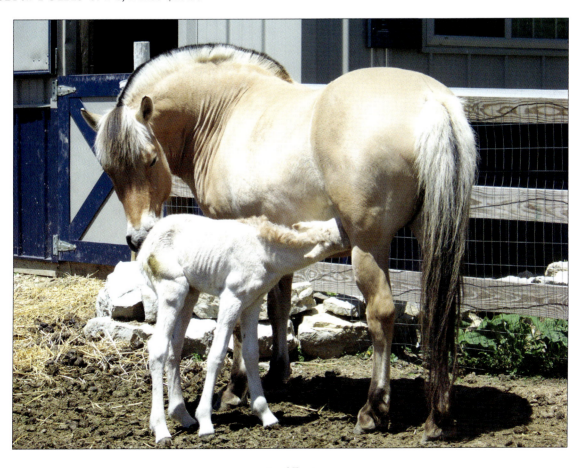

*Annie is a retired Speech and Language Pathologist, who taught for thirty-two years in the Stoughton, Wisconsin public schools. Stoughton is well known for its "Syttende Mai" celebration, which commemorates the Norwegian Independence Day. Annie's Norwegian-American heritage and her love of folktales has led her to write her own Scandinavian tales. She still enjoys visiting schools to do presentations related to writing and publishing for elementary students.*

*Contact information:* **annies49@yahoo.com** *Subject: school visits.*

*Annie Jacobsen is the author of four Scandinavian folktales for children of all ages. Her works include:* **"The Terrible Troll Cat," "Ivar, The Short But Brave, Viking," "Hang On If You Want To Come Along!"** *and her latest 2009 release,* **"The Tale of the Troll's Horse."**

*These delightful books are available at:* **www.pickledherringpress.com** *and through Baker & Taylor.*

*Susan has been drawing, painting, potting, carving, metal smithing and sculpting all her life. This multi-media experience has prepared her for almost any commission.*

*Susan keeps her interest in art vibrant with studies at the Art Institute of Chicago, and continuous learning at various other institutions and classes. She holds a BFA from the U of I. Susan has had the benefit and joy of lifelong tutelage under her father, artist Robert Hanson.*

*Her love of animals includes rescued cats, dogs, and horses, plus a love of the outdoors makes it fun for her to develop the story in pictures. Susan's pride in her Norwegian heritage can be seen in her illustrations. She credits her family and friends for her inspiration.*

*Photo courtesy of Yahara River Fjords*
*Karen and Stuart Hanson*

*Robert Hanson received his Fine Arts degree from the University of Wisconsin.*

*He had a long and distinguished career as an illustrator and commercial artist in Chicago. He specialized in portraiture, but is truly a multimedia artist. He is a patient, kind, and skilled instructor. Robert is enjoying life with his wife, Arlene, and dear friends back in his home town of Stoughton, Wisconsin. He still paints in his studio every day.*

*He and Annie's father have been friends since fourth grade. What a treasure he is to all of us!*

*With much love,*

*Annie and Susan*

*Dear Suzi,*

*We've known each other for so many years.*
*We've shared adventures, secrets, laughter and tears.*
*You must know how very special you are to me,*
*Just as you know, friends forever we will be!*

*With love and gratitude,*

*Annie*

**The End!**